First American Edition 2010
Kane Miller, A Division of EDC Publishing

First published in the Netherlands in 2009 by Standaard Uitgeverij nv
under the title, "Zoekboek, Rik bij de dieren."
Copyright © 2009 Standaard Uitgeverij nv

For information contact:
Kane Miller, A Division of EDC Publishing
P.O. Box 470663
Tulsa, OK 74147-0663
www.kanemiller.com
www.edcpub.com

Library of Congress Control Number: 2009932553

Manufactured by Regent Publishing Services, Hong Kong
Printed September 2010 in ShenZhen, Guangdong, China
1 2 3 4 5 6 7 8 9 10

ISBN: 978-1-935279-35-8

Liesbet Slegers

Andy and Sam

Hide-and-Seek

Hello! I'm Andy, and this is my cat Sam.

Sometimes Sam is a bit naughty. He likes to hide.

Can you help me find him?

There are some other questions for you, too ...

Kane Miller
A DIVISION OF EDC PUBLISHING

IN THE HOUSE

This is my house.
I like animals a lot. Do you?

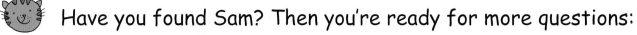 Have you found Sam? Then you're ready for more questions:

- How many pets does Andy have? Don't forget to count Sam!
- Do you see the spider? Is *he* a pet?

○ Look out, fish! Somebody's watching you! Who is it?

● Andy has a present for Mom. Where did he hide it?

○ Grandma brought three candies. Can you find them?

THE BACKYARD

I love to play outside.
I especially love to play with my dog.
There are lots of other animals in my
backyard too ...

Have you found Sam? Then you're ready for more questions:

○ Which tiny animal has his house on his back?

○ Where's the chicken? And the rabbit?

○ The bird has a worm. Who do you think it's for?

◉ Can you help Andy's dog find his bone?

○ Who lives underground?

IN THE SKY

This is my treehouse.
I'm as tall as the treetops and high in the sky!
Look at all the birds.

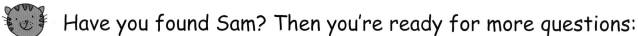 Have you found Sam? Then you're ready for more questions:

- How many animals are flying? (Sam counts as one too.)
- How many things are flying that are *not* animals?

- Which bird is the most colorful?
- Who built a nest?
- Where is Andy's other shoe?

BY THE POND

I'm fishing with Dad.
My line is in the water.
Now we're waiting for the fish to bite.

Have you found Sam? Then you're ready for more questions:

- The rowboat is missing a paddle. Where is it?
- There are four dragonflies. Can you find them?

- Quack! Quack! Who isn't in line?
- Who is sticking out his tongue to catch a fly?
- How many frogs are there?

IN THE WOODS

We're having a picnic.
Mom brought lots of food.
Yum!

Have you found Sam? Then you're ready for more questions:
- Find the ants. What are they doing?
- What did Sam bring in case it rains?

○ Who is taking a nap?

● How many rabbits are there?

○ Which mommy just found her baby?

ON THE FARM

The farm is a very busy place.
Chicken, cows, horses, sheep ...
They're all my friends!

Have you found Sam? Then you're ready for more questions:

- Where is the brown cow? Where's the black and white one?
- What is keeping the birds away from the vegetables?

○ Who is hiding behind the bush?

● Who belongs in the pond?

○ Can you find the white chicken?

THE HENHOUSE

The farmer built a little house just for the chickens.
They like to sleep and lay their eggs there.
I like to help feed them. I brought them some corn.

 Have you found Sam? Then you're ready for more questions:

○ What did Andy find? Where did they come from?

○ How many baby chicks are there?

How many chickens are still sleeping?

Who is eating corn, but is not a chicken?

Where did Sam put his ball?

ON THE BEACH

I like to visit the beach in the summer.
I play in the sand and look for shells.
Look at my beautiful sandcastle.

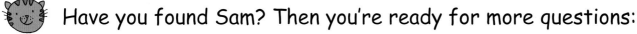 Have you found Sam? Then you're ready for more questions:
- Who is tickling Mom's foot?
- Can you spot the seal?

- How many boats are in the water?
- **Which is the biggest animal?**
- Do you see any birds on the sand?

AT THE ZOO

You can see lots of different animals at the zoo.
I like the crocodiles and the monkeys.
Which do you like best?

Have you found Sam? Then you're ready for more questions:

- How many elephants do you see?
- What is the monkey eating?

- What is Andy doing?
- Can you find the rabbit?
- Which giraffe has the longest neck?

LUNCHTIME AT THE ZOO

The penguins are waddling around.
The tiger is in his cage.
And I'm having my lunch.

 Have you found Sam? Then you're ready for more questions:

- Who moves very, very slowly?
- Which animals like the cold?

- Where is the parrot?
- Who is riding in his mother's pouch?
- How many penguins are there?

HOME AGAIN

I am very tired.
It's time for bed.
My room has all of my favorite things.
Good night, friends!

Have you found Sam? Then you're ready for more questions:
- Who does Andy like to cuddle?
- Where does he keep his shells from the beach?

- Whose pictures are on the wall?
- How many mice are on the curtain?
- Where does the guinea pig sleep?

IN THE HOUSE

THE BACKYARD

IN THE SKY

BY THE POND

IN THE WOODS

ON THE FARM

THE HENHOUSE

ON THE BEACH

AT THE ZOO

LUNCHTIME AT THE ZOO

HOME AGAIN